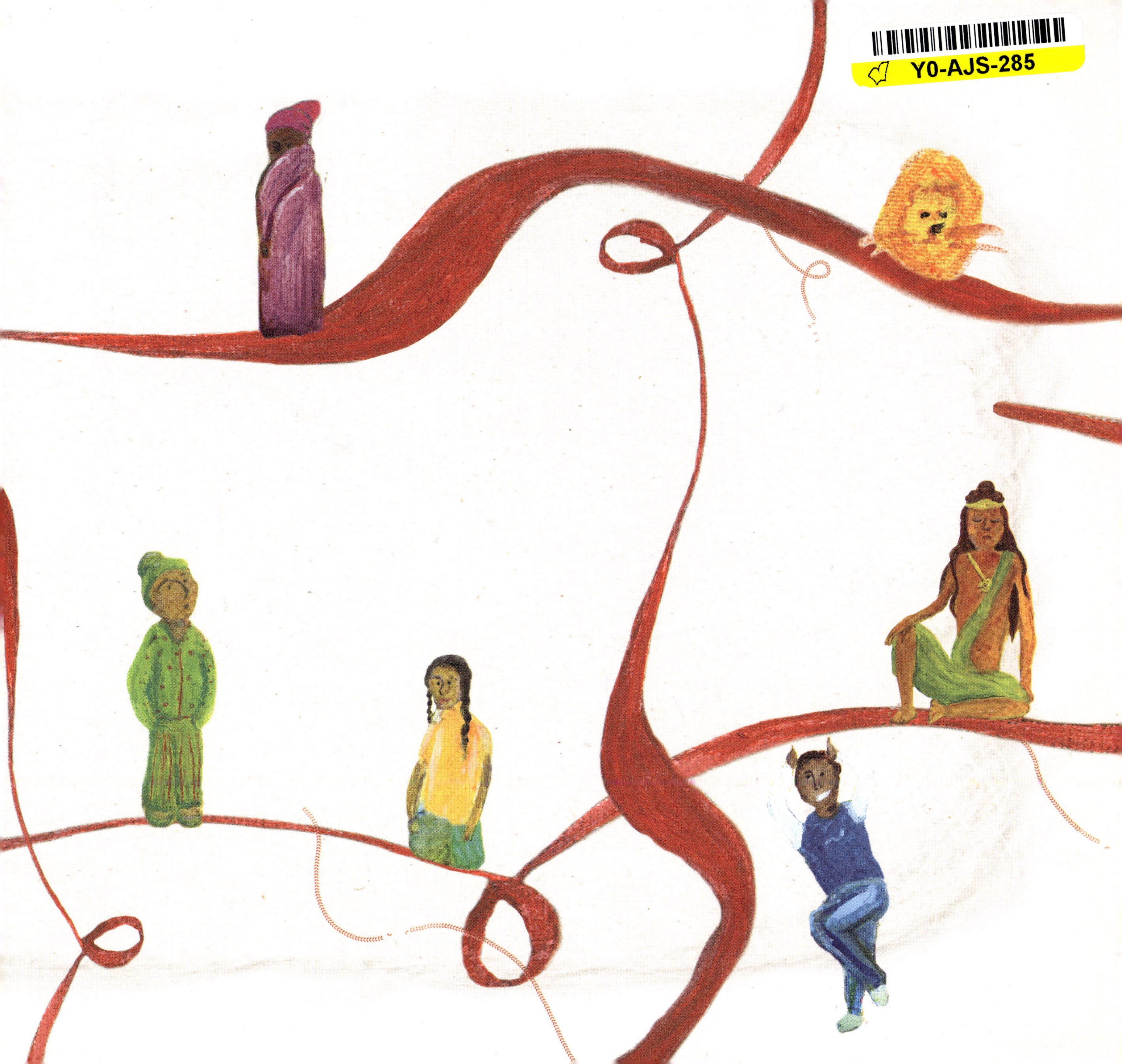

*For all the lioness
and lion cubs roaring for change.
Be different. Be You.* – N

For Sonia – J

Text Copyright © 2009 by Navjot Kaur
Illustrations Copyright © 2009 by Jaspreet Sandhu
Published in Canada by Saffron Press

All rights reserved.
Thank you for complying with copyright laws. No part of this book may be reproduced, stored in a retrieval system or transmitted, in any form or by any means (known or hereby invented), without prior written consent of the publisher.

Revised Edition 2019
4 6 8 10 9 7 5 3

Design by Studio L-E
The illustrations were prepared using acrylic on canvas

Library and Archives Canada Cataloguing in Publication
Kaur, Navjot
A lion's mane / Navjot Kaur ; illustrator: Jaspreet Sandhu.
ISBN 978-0-9812412-0-3
    1. Turbans--Religious aspects--Sikhism--Juvenile literature.
    2. Sikhs--Ethnic identity--Juvenile literature.
    I. Sandhu, Jaspreet   II. Title.
BL2018.5.T87K38 2009   j294.6'446   C2009-902893-X

Printed and bound in China on FSC assured paper

SAFFRON PRESS
Order at www.saffronpress.com

A Lion's Mane

STORY BY
Navjot Kaur

ILLUSTRATED BY
Jaspreet Sandhu

I have a lion's mane
and I am different, just like you.

Do you know who I am?

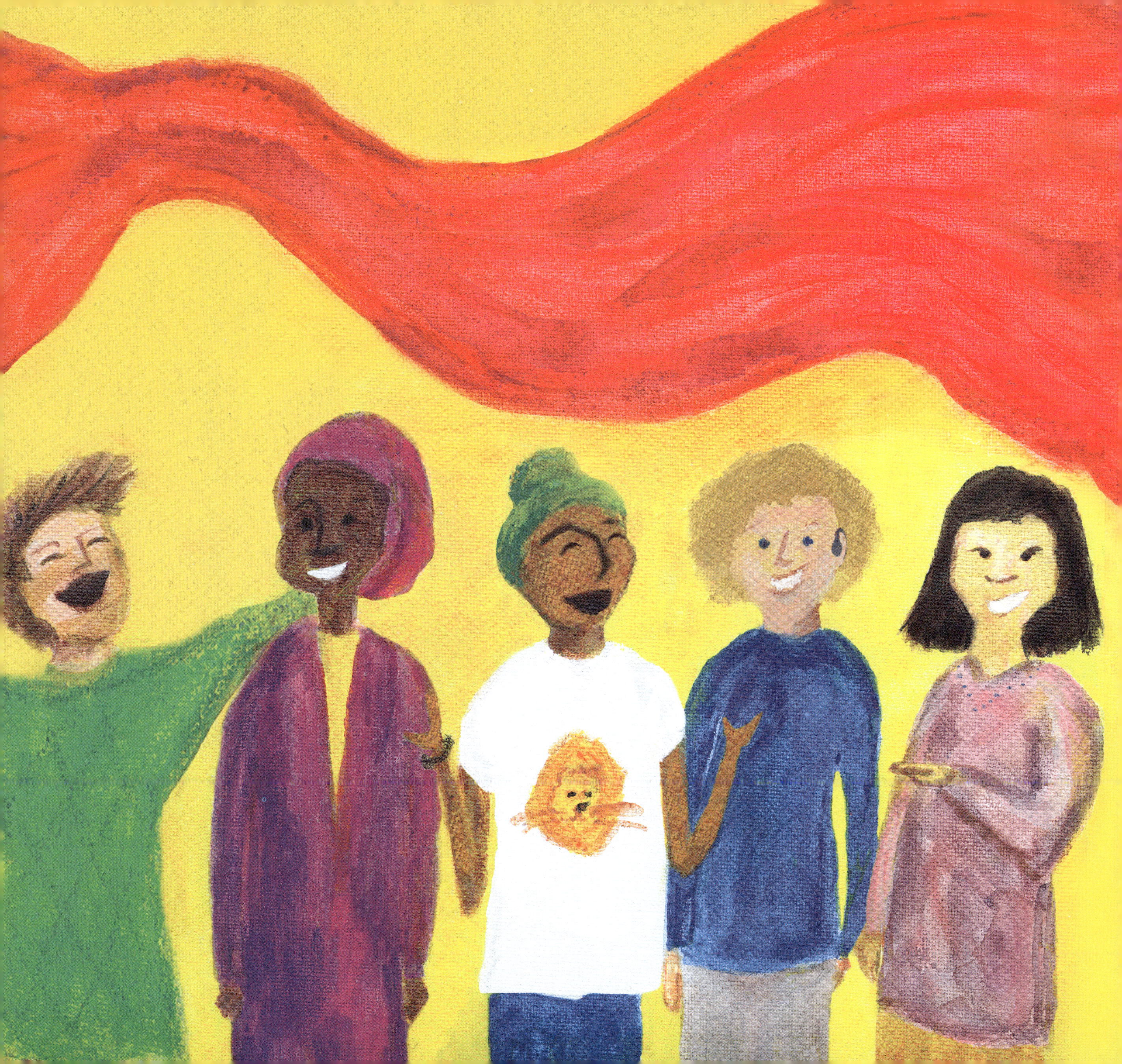

Lions are celebrated in many cultures around the world.

Join my flowing
red *dastaar* on a journey
to discover
why *I* have a lion's mane.

Have you heard of *Simba*?

king *strong*

Look deeply into
what covers my mane to see
what *simba* means in *Kiswahili*
– the *Bantu* language.

Simba is the Swahili word for lion.

I have to be strong
when people don't know who I am.

SWAHILI

admire respect

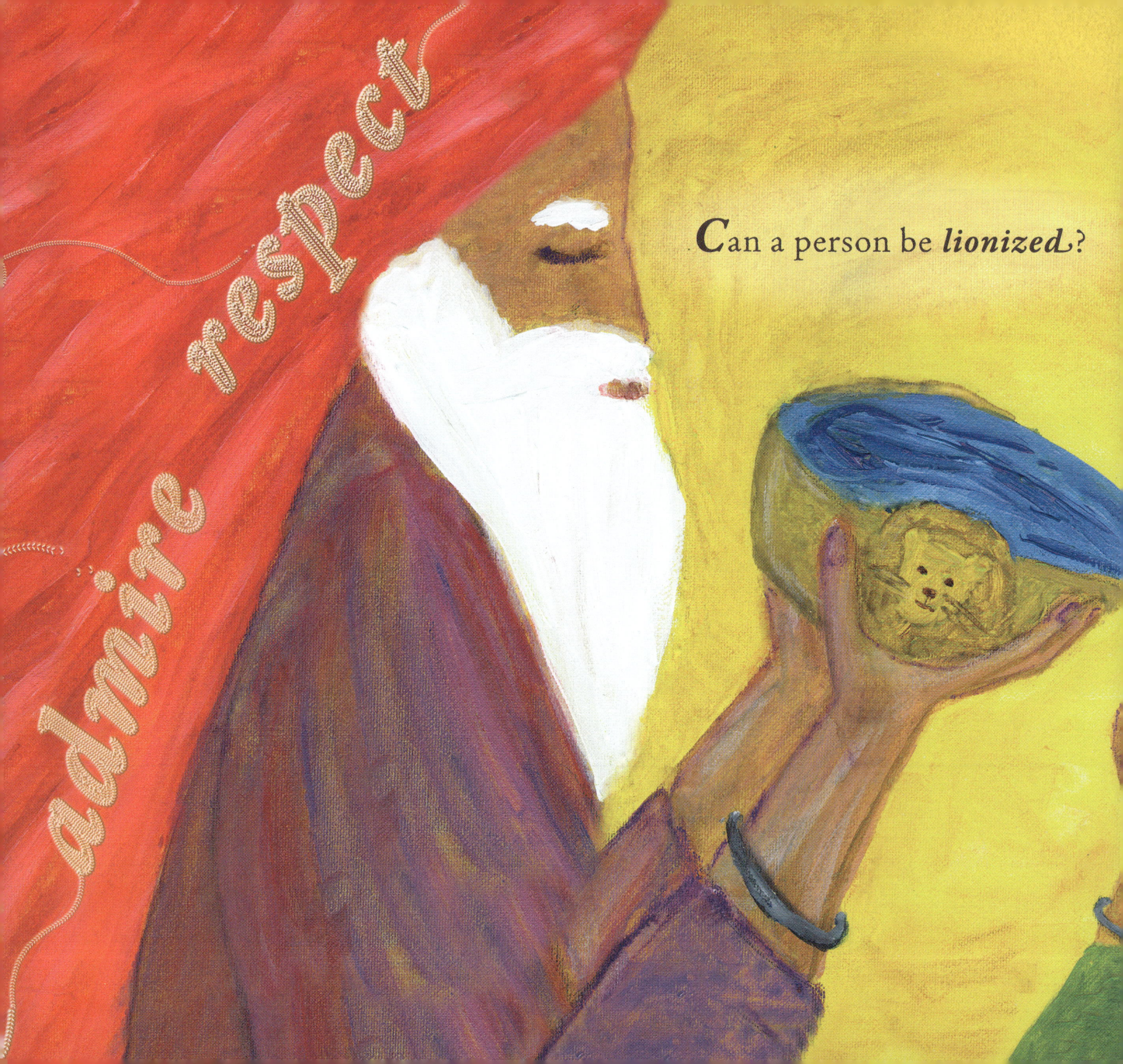

Can a person be *lionized*?

Look deeply into
what covers my mane to see
what *lionize* means.

I admire my Nana ji.
His stories tell of mighty lionesses
and Khalsa knights,
who stand up for what is right,
even when it is hard to do.

𝒜 medieval king was given the name *lionheart*.

Look deeply into
what covers my mane to see
what *lionhearted* means.

Being a Khalsa knight gives me
the courage to stand up to bullies.

courageous

brave

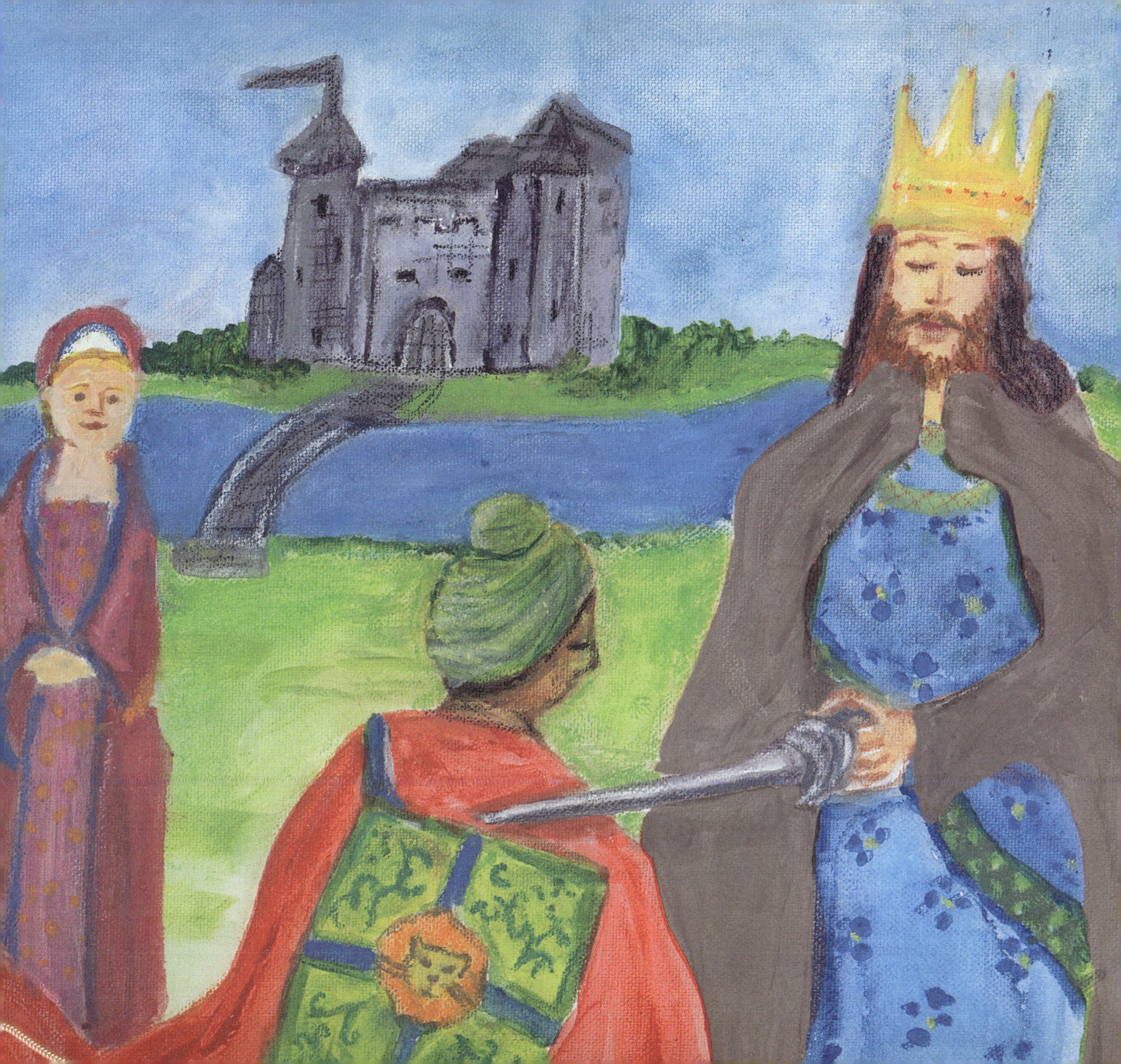

Can a *lioness* take charge, too?

Of course she can!

loyalty   survival

Look deeply into
what covers my mane to see
what is important to her.

Wangari Maathai and **Q**ueen Rania
have worked hard
to create change in our world.

My sister has the roar of a lioness!
She is always helping to plant strong ideas.

What happens when one lion roars?

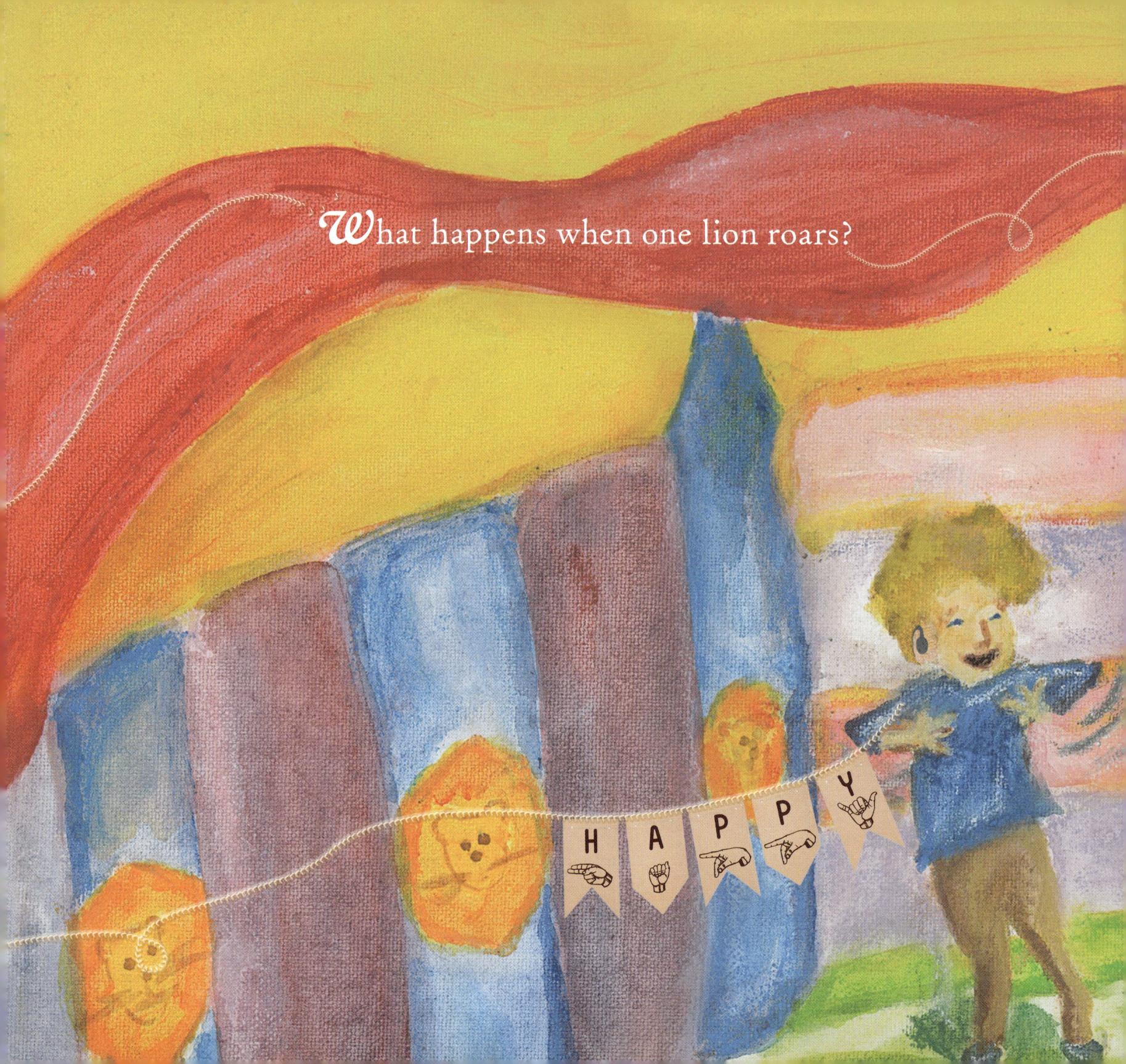

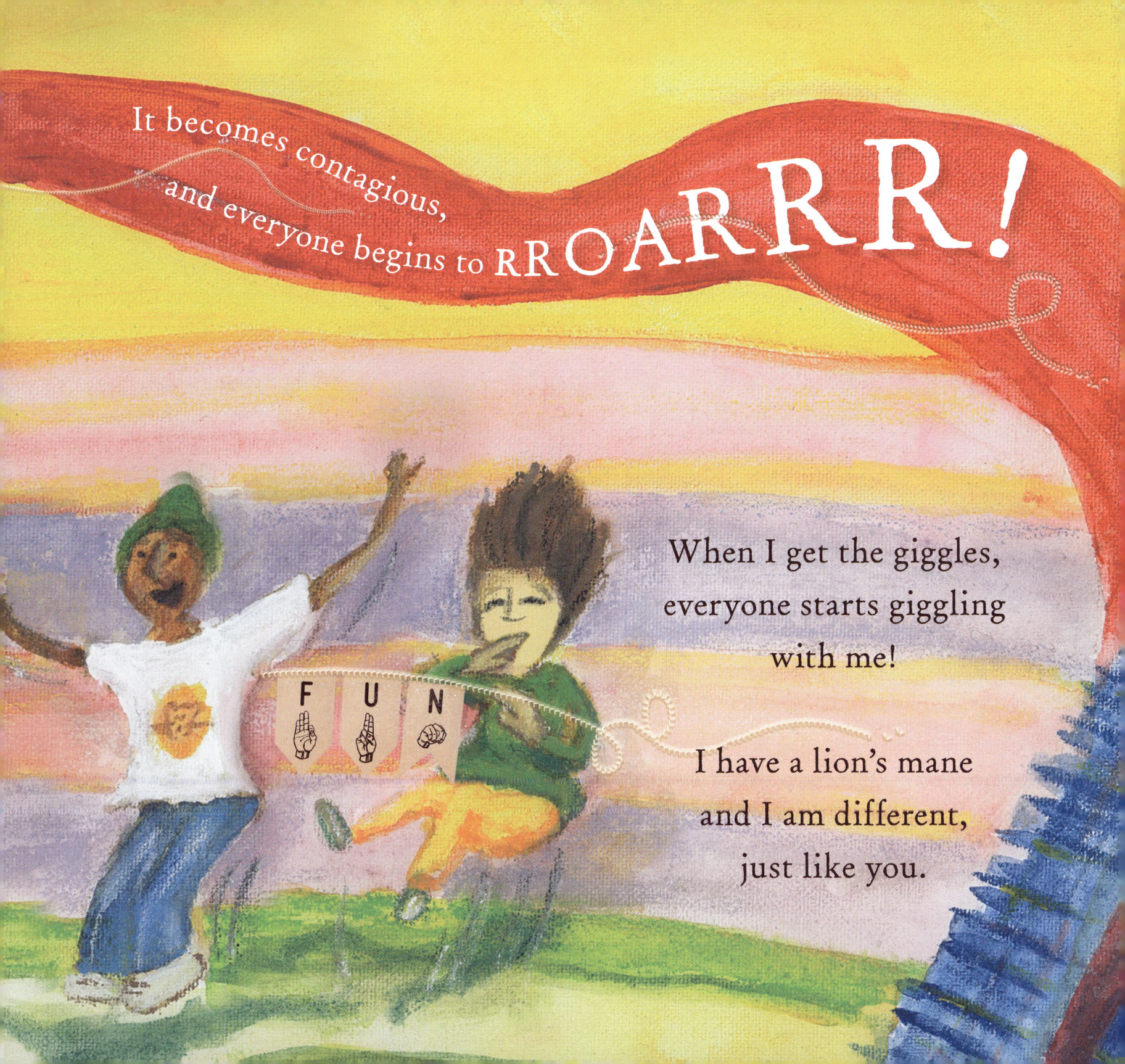

It becomes contagious, and everyone begins to RROARRR!

When I get the giggles, everyone starts giggling with me!

I have a lion's mane and I am different, just like you.

In ancient Iran,
the mountains and plains of the FARS province
were filled with lion mines,
until the lions became ex t i n c t.

Using fine woolen threads, weavers
created lion rugs to celebrate bravery.

Look deeply into
what covers my mane to see
what the lion means to
the Iranian people.

It is hard to be patient sometimes,
but I see people being kind and
taking turns when they are doing *seva*
– serving food in our community kitchens –
the *Langar*.

generosity

patience

LANGAR

Can you guess
what *simha* means?

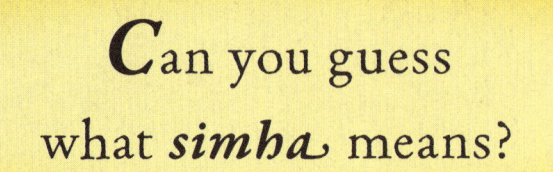

In the Sanskrit language,
simha means the same as my last name.

singh, simba & simha

Look deeply into
what covers my mane to see
how these words belong together.

mean ... lion!

The *simha-sa-na* yoga pose
is like a lion taking a deep breath.
It makes me feel brave.

Wenshu was
the ancient bodhi-sattva of wisdom.
He wore his long mane
in five hair buns on his head.

Look deeply into
what covers my mane to see
what the lion meant for him.

wisdom

power

I look *different*,
so some people make fun of me.

It takes wisdom to use our words
and explain who we are.
When we learn something new,
it makes each of us stronger.

WENSHU

*H*ave you ever watched the movements
of the Lion Dance
during many Chinese celebrations?

Long ago, martial artists copied the way
animals moved in nature.

Look deeply into
what covers my mane to see
why the *Kung-Fu* artists
copied the lion.

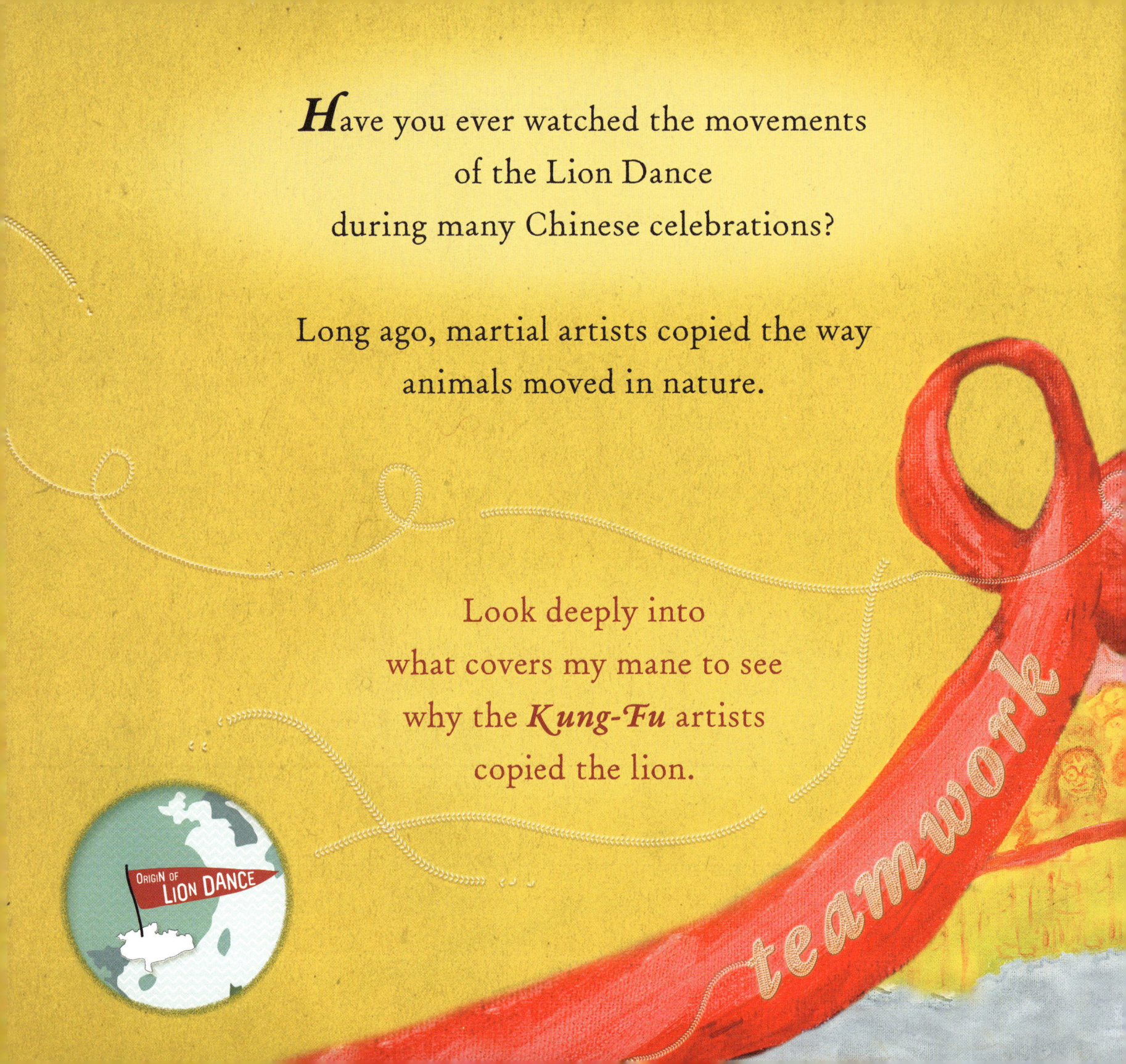

ORIGIN OF LION DANCE

team work

Gatka is a form of
martial art practiced since the time of my ancestors.

I hope I can try it one day.

The mountain lion
is profoundly sacred to the *Hopi* people.

Look deeply into
what covers my mane to see
why they respect the lion.

guidance

My dastaar guides me
to make good choices every day.

HOPI NATION

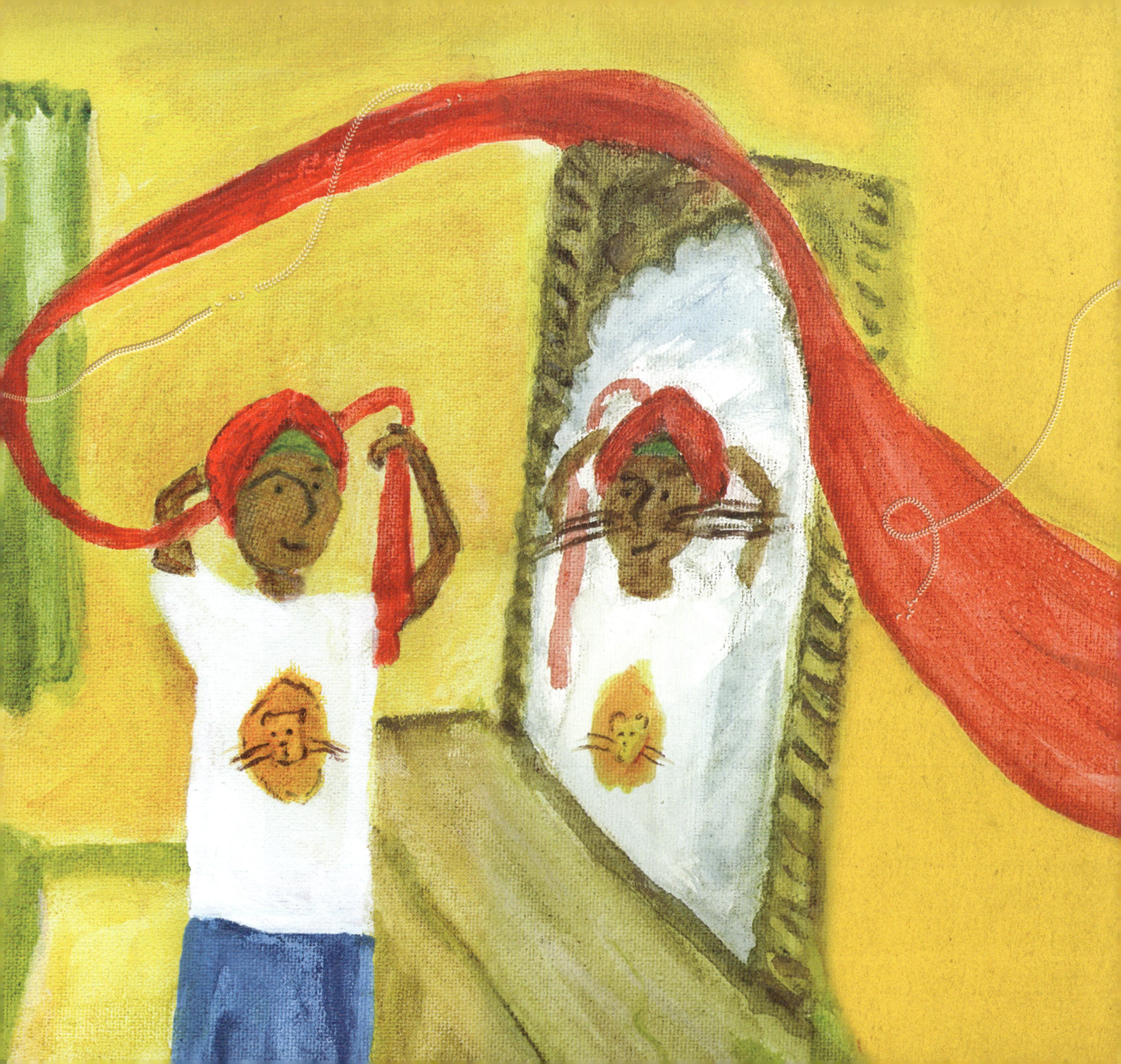

A Lion's Mane can also offer **protection**

I feel safe and sure with my lion's mane.

My mane shares
a connection with so many cultures
around the world.

I have a lion's mane.
I am a Singh.
I am a Sikh.
And I am happy to be different,
just like you!

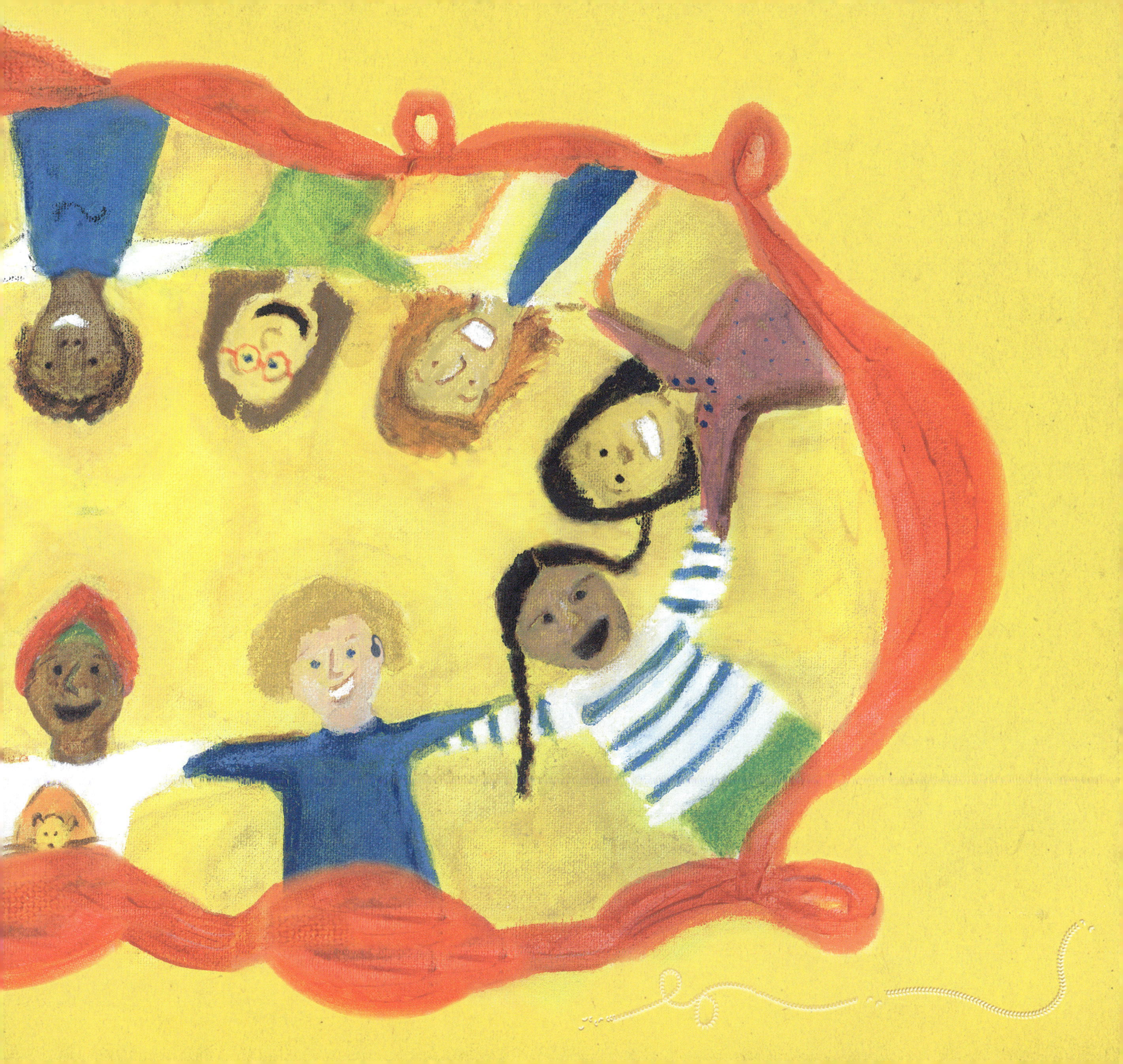

Glossary & Pronunciation Guide

03.
Fars (Province)
/ faar-ss /
‡
Originally Pars - one of the 30 provinces of Iran. Immigrants of Zoroastrian heritage are still known as Parsees today.

02.
Dastaar
/ dah-star /
‡
Describes the fabric tied into a turban. Members of the Sikh community wear a dastaar as a daily action of their faith.

01.
Bodhisattva
/ bo-dhee-sahth-vah /
‡
In Buddhism, a Bodhisattva is someone who shares and looks for kindness in every being.

05.
Hopi
/ hō-pē /
‡
The Hopi, or People of Peace, are an Indigenous nation, located in northeastern Arizona.

06.
Khalsa
/ khal-sah /
‡
A nation created in Anandpur 1699. Upstanders: to stand up for what is right, even when it is hard to do. They follow teachings of the Sikh faith.

04.
Gatka
/ gat-th-ka /
‡
A martial art form practised by members of the Sikh community. It also refers to the stick used during Gatka.

07.
Kiswahili
/ kee-swa-hee-lee /
‡
Kiswahili is a Bantu language spoken in Southeast Africa.
Prefix: ki (from)
Root: sawahil (coast)
Kiswahili: language of the coast

08.
Kung-fu
/ khang-foo /
‡
A Chinese martial art form Includes different styles that were created over the centuries.

09.
Langar
/ lun-gur /
‡
A (mobile) kitchen serving vegetarian food and run by members of the Sikh community.
Langar was started 500 years ago with a goal to end hunger and create equity within communities.

10. Nana ji
/ nah-nah-jee /

‡

An endearing name for one's maternal grandfather.

11. Queen Rania
/ raa –ni-ah /

‡

Queen of Jordan.
Strong advocate for education locally and around the world Challenges stereotypes of Muslims and Arabs through her work.

12. Sanskrit
/ sun-skrit /

‡

An ancient language, which has influenced most modern languages of India and Nepal.

13. Seva
/ say-vah /

‡

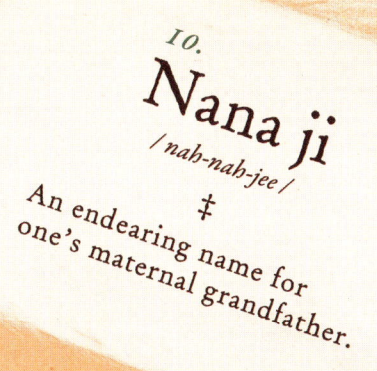

Seva is like sharing random acts of kindness – you do them without anyone knowing it was you.

14. Sikh
/ si-kh /

‡

Sikh means to learn.
Sikhi or Sikhism is the fifth largest religion in the world, originating in northern India. Members of this community identify as Sikhs.

15. Simha-sana
/ sim-aa-sa-na /

‡

In Sanskrit, simha means the powerful one and is also the word for lion. In yoga, it is a pose that looks and sounds like a roaring lion.

16. Singh
/ si-ng-h /

‡

Singh means lion.
Common last names for members of the Sikh community remove the prejudice of social labels.
Kaur = lioness, Singh = lion
The name offered people the right to stand in their own truth.

17. Wangari Maathai
(1940-2011)

/ wan-gah-ree, maa-thai /

‡

An environmental and political activist from Kenya who was awarded the Nobel Peace Prize in 2004.

18. Wenshu
/ wen-shoo /

‡

Also known as Manjuri, Wenshu is the Bodhisattva of Wisdom or Protector of Learning.
He is usually shown seated on a white or blue lion. He holds a sword in his right hand (to cut through ignorance) and either the stem of a lotus or a pile of books in his left (to show how important it is to keep learning).

FIND ALL THE PLACES

HOPI NATION

Atlantic Ocean

Add flags to show the story of how you are different, just like me.

FROM A LION·MA

- QUEEN RANIA
- FARS PROVINCE
- WENSHU
- LANGAR
- WANGARI MAATHAI
- ORIGIN OF LION DANCE
- SWAHILI

Pacific Ocean

Indian Ocean

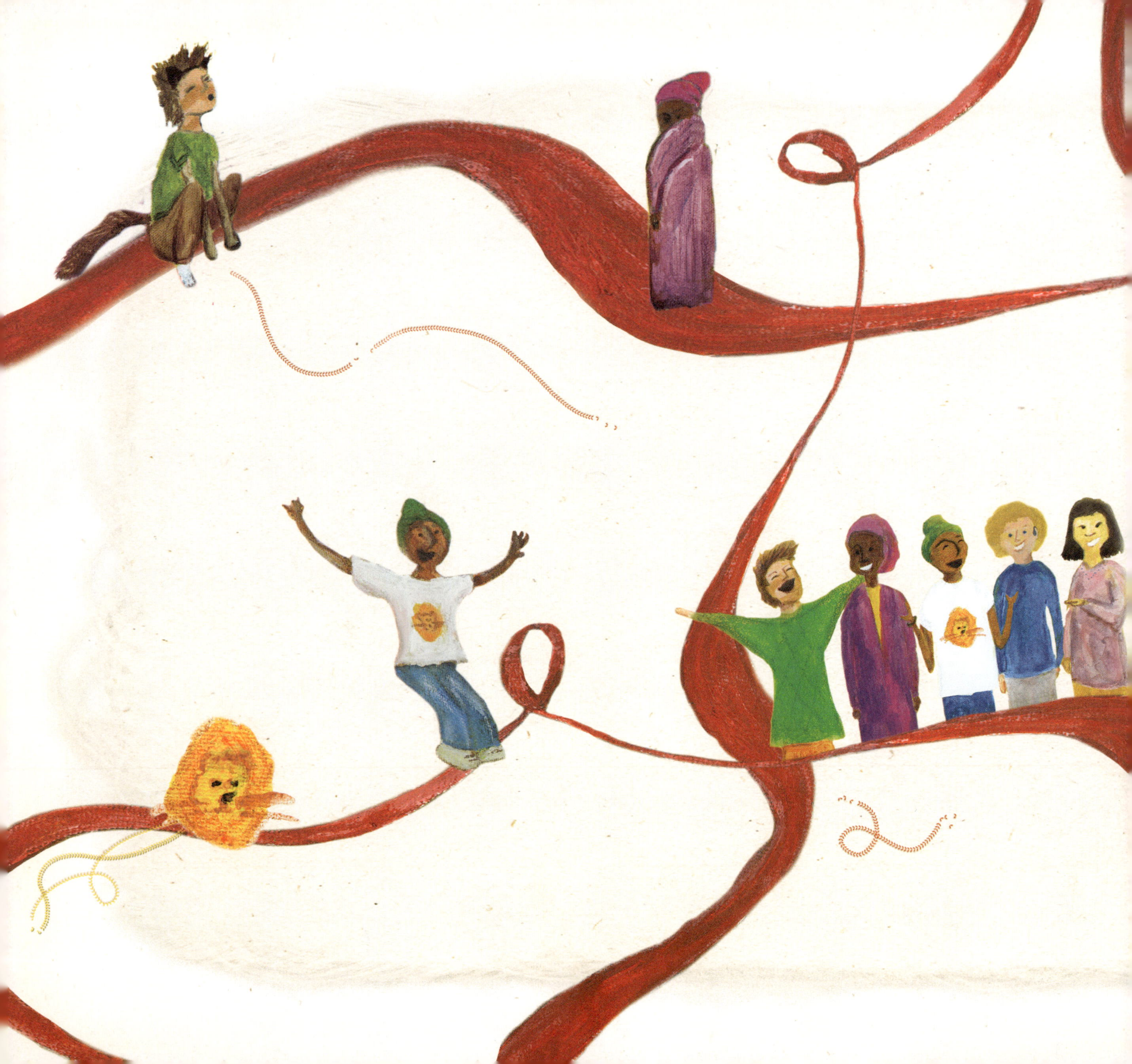